S0-BAA-297

OH, CRUMPS!

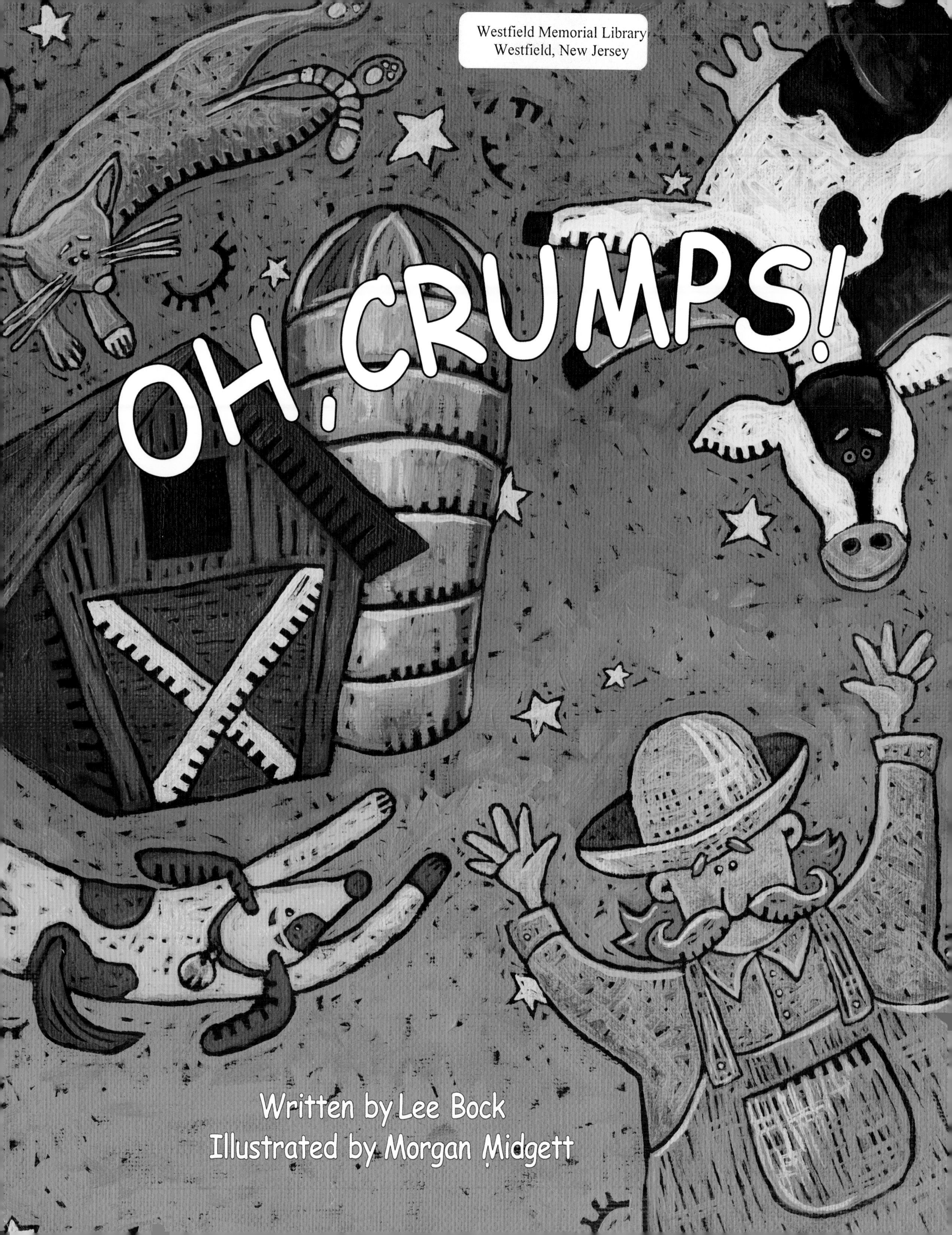

Written by Lee Bock

Illustrated by Morgan Midgett

To Bob, whose morning always comes early.

⌒⋉ Lee

Many thanks to Lee, for giving me the opportunity to work with a truly gifted and inspirational storyteller.

⌒⋉ Morgan

Bock, Lee.

    Oh, crumps! / written by Lee Bock ; illustrated by Morgan Midgett–1st ed.–McHenry, IL: Raven Tree Press, 2009.

    p. ; cm.

    SUMMARY: The misadventures of a sleepy farmer as he agonizes over a mixed-up list of the coming day's chores. How will he ever milk the fence, repair the cow, mow the silo and climb the hay before morning comes?

English–Only Edition
ISBN 978-1-934960-70-7 hardcover

Bilingual Edition
ISBN 978-0-972019-24-8 hardcover
ISBN 978-0-9770906-3-1 paperback

Audience: Ages 4-8
Title available in English-only or bilingual English-Spanish editions

1. Domestic animals–Juvenile fiction. 2. Farm life–Juvenile fiction. 3. Animal sounds–Juvenile fiction.
[1.] Domestic animals–Fiction. [2.] Farm life–Fiction. [3.] Animal sounds–Fiction. I. Midgett, Morgan. II. Title.

LCCN: 2009923417

Printed in Taiwan
10 9 8 7 6 5 4 3 2 1

First Edition

Free activities for this book are available at www.raventreepress.com

OH, CRUMPS!

Written by Lee Bock

Illustrated by Morgan Midgett

Raven Tree Press
A Division of Delta Systems Co., Inc.
www.raventreepress.com

One summer night, Farmer Felandro went to bed early. He pulled the blanket up under his nose and yawned.

"I'm soooo tired. I can hardly think. Tomorrow will be a busy day. I have to milk the cows, fix the fence, mow the hay, and climb the silo. Morning comes early," he said. Then he closed his sleepy eyes.

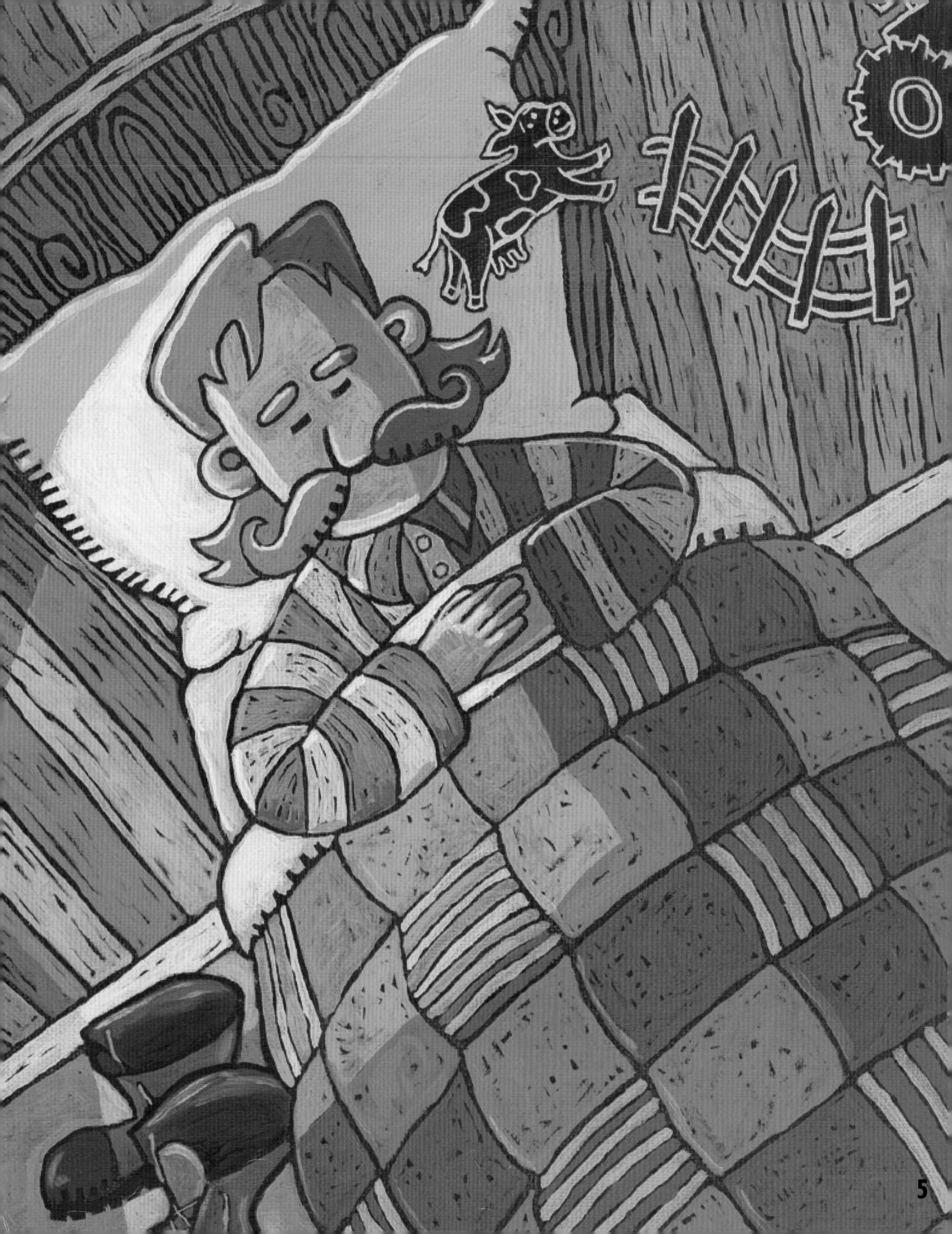

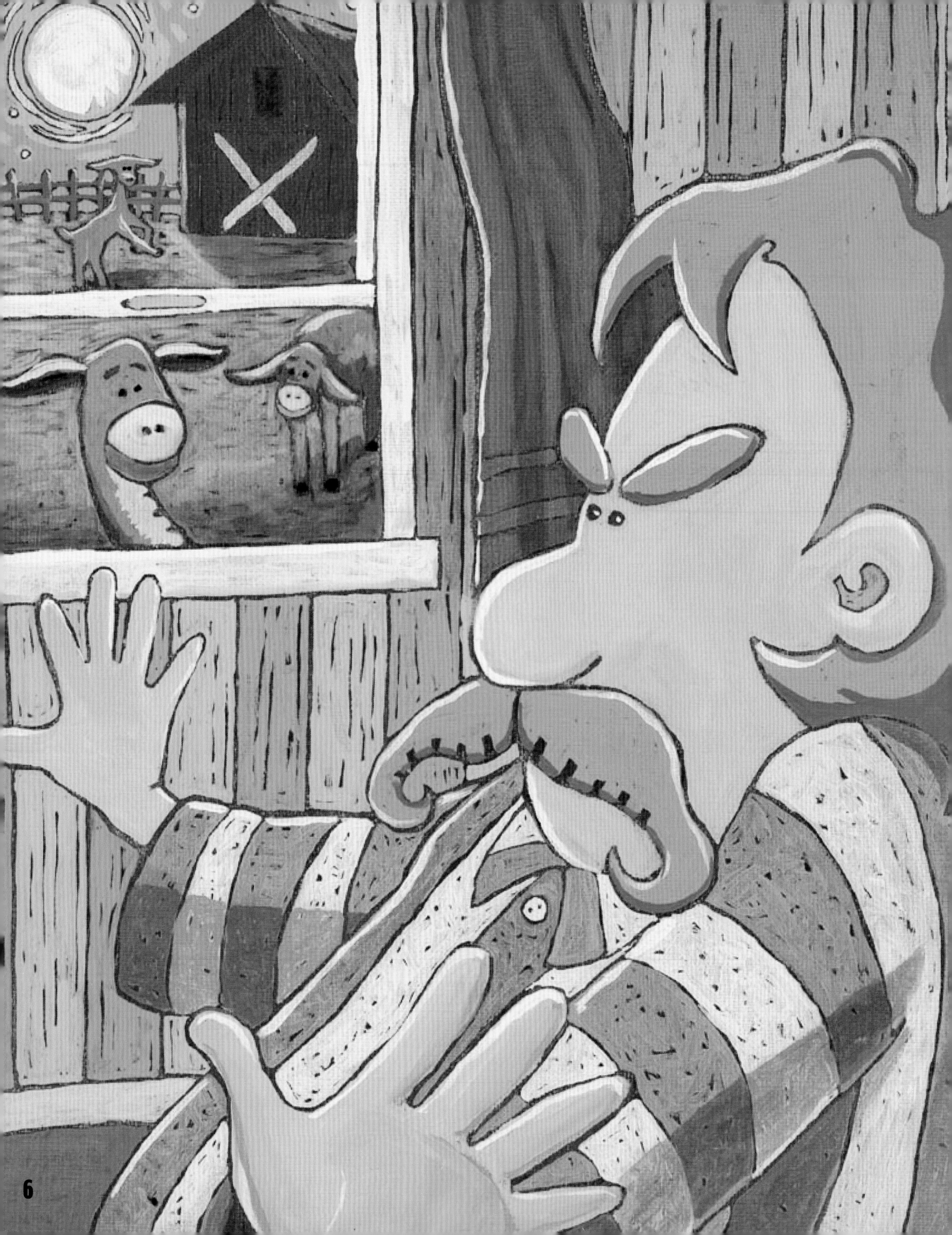

Maaaa! Maaaa! Maaaaaah!

Farmer Felandro sat up. "What's that noise?" he grumbled. Then he remembered: "Oh, crumps! I forgot to put the kids to bed."

So the farmer stuck his feet into his old brown work boots and clumpidy clumped down the steps. He slammed the screen door on his way out and chased the three little goats into their pen behind the barn.

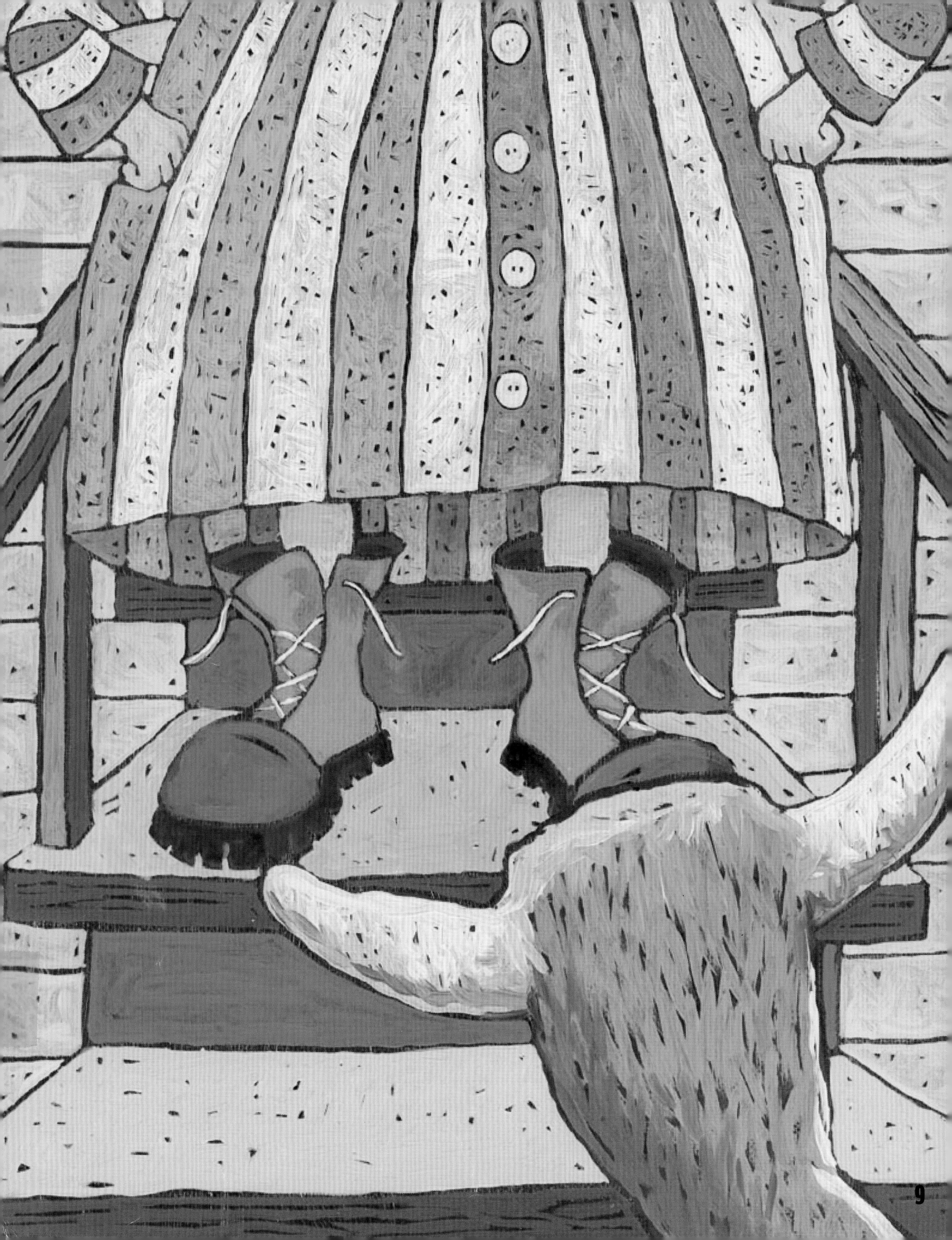

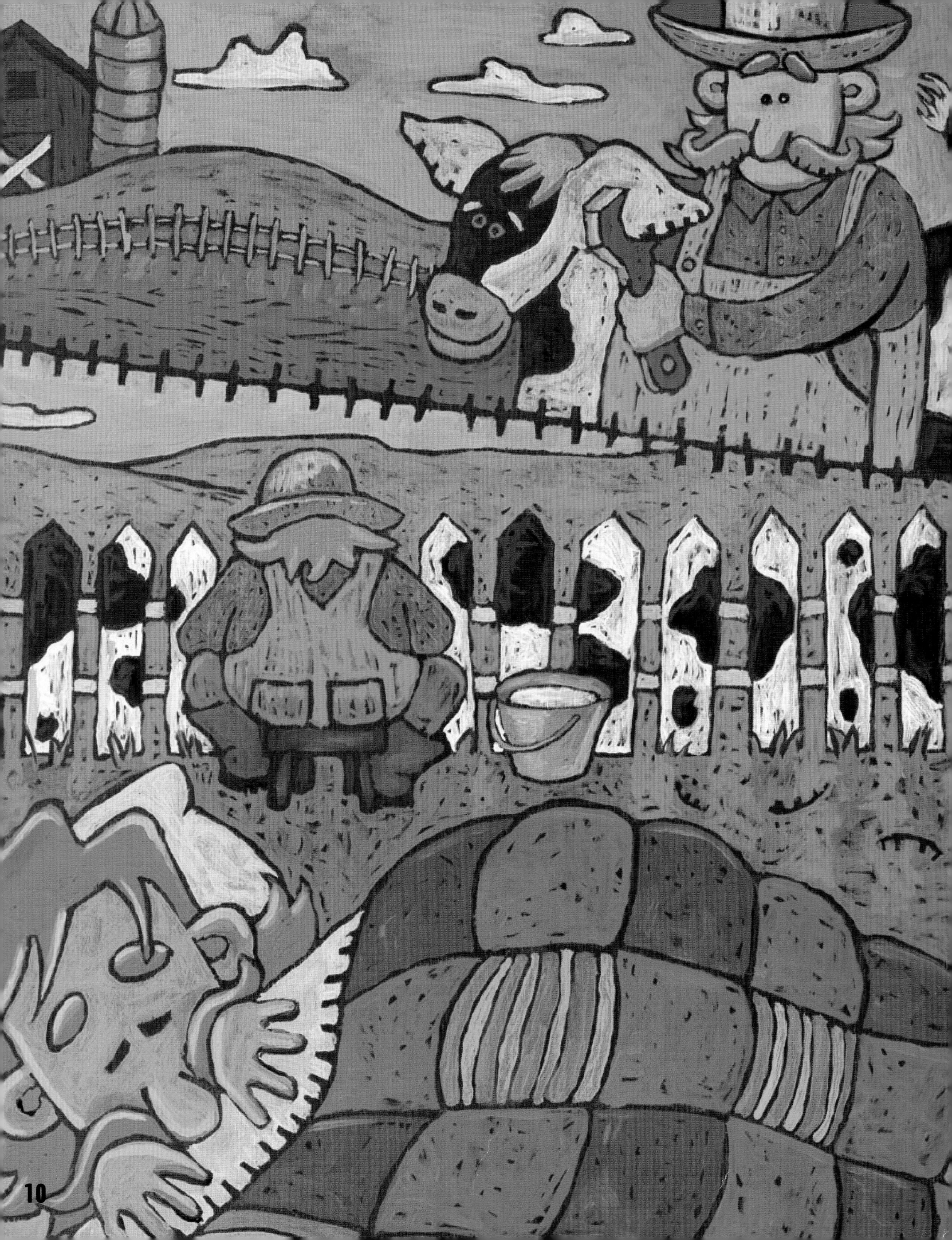

"Now it's quiet, and I can get some sleep." When he got back into bed, he pulled the blanket up under his nose and yawned.

"I'm soooo tired. I can hardly think. Tomorrow will be a busy day. I have to fix the cow, milk the fence, mow the hay, and climb the silo. Morning comes early." Then he closed his sleepy eyes.

Brrrrruffff ruff ruff! Brrrrruffff! Brrrrruffff ruff!

Farmer Felandro sat up. "What's that noise?" he grumbled. Then he remembered: "Oh, crumps! I woke up the dogs when I slammed the screen door. Now they will bark all night long."

So the farmer stuck his feet into his old brown work boots and clumpidy clumped down the steps. He closed the screen door carefully on his way out and chased the two big dogs into the hayloft.

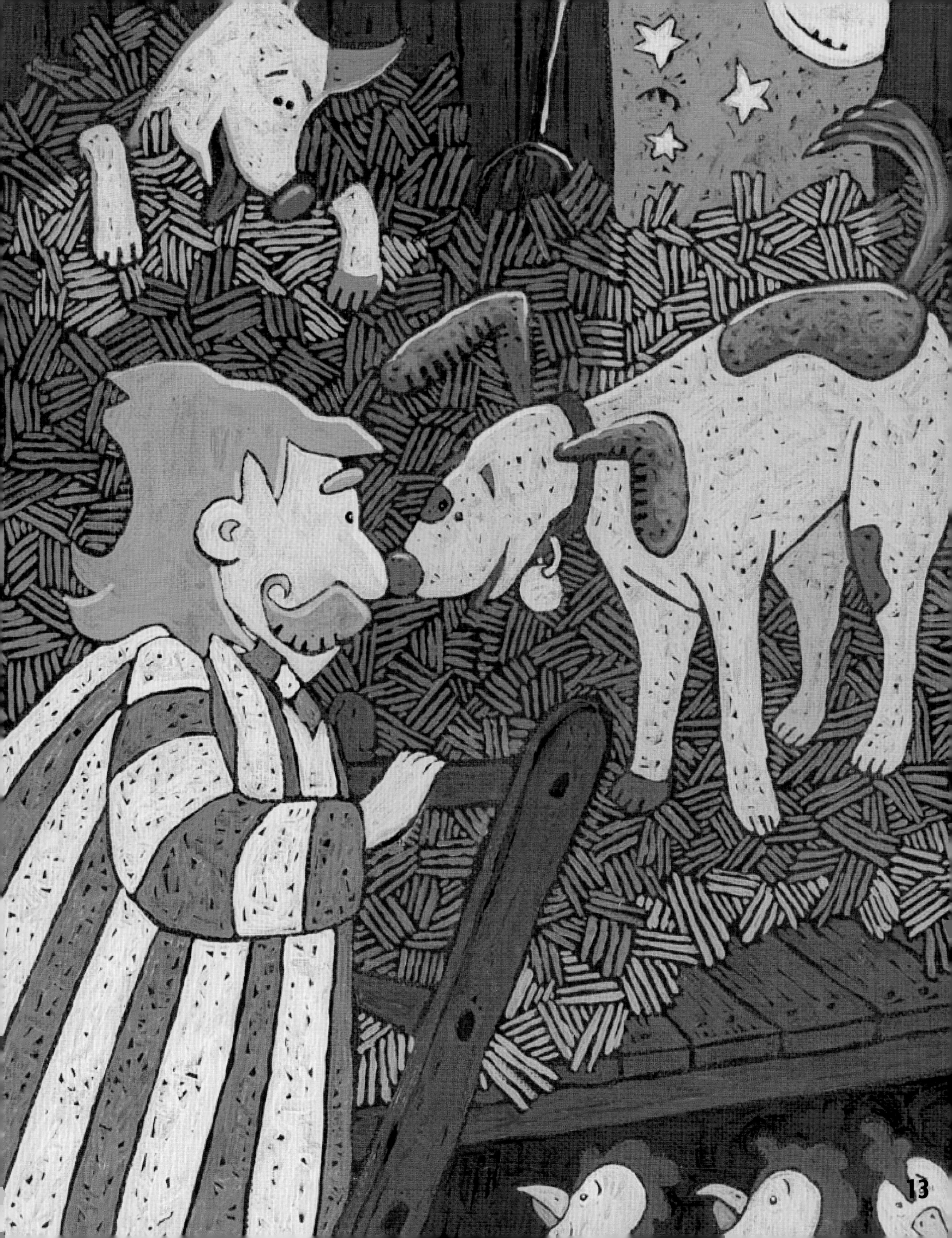

"Now it's quiet, and I can get some sleep." When he got back into bed, he pulled the blanket up under his nose and yawned.

"I am soooo tired. I can hardly think. Tomorrow will be a busy day. I have to mow the cow, climb the fence, fix the hay, and milk the silo. Morning comes early." Then he closed his sleepy eyes.

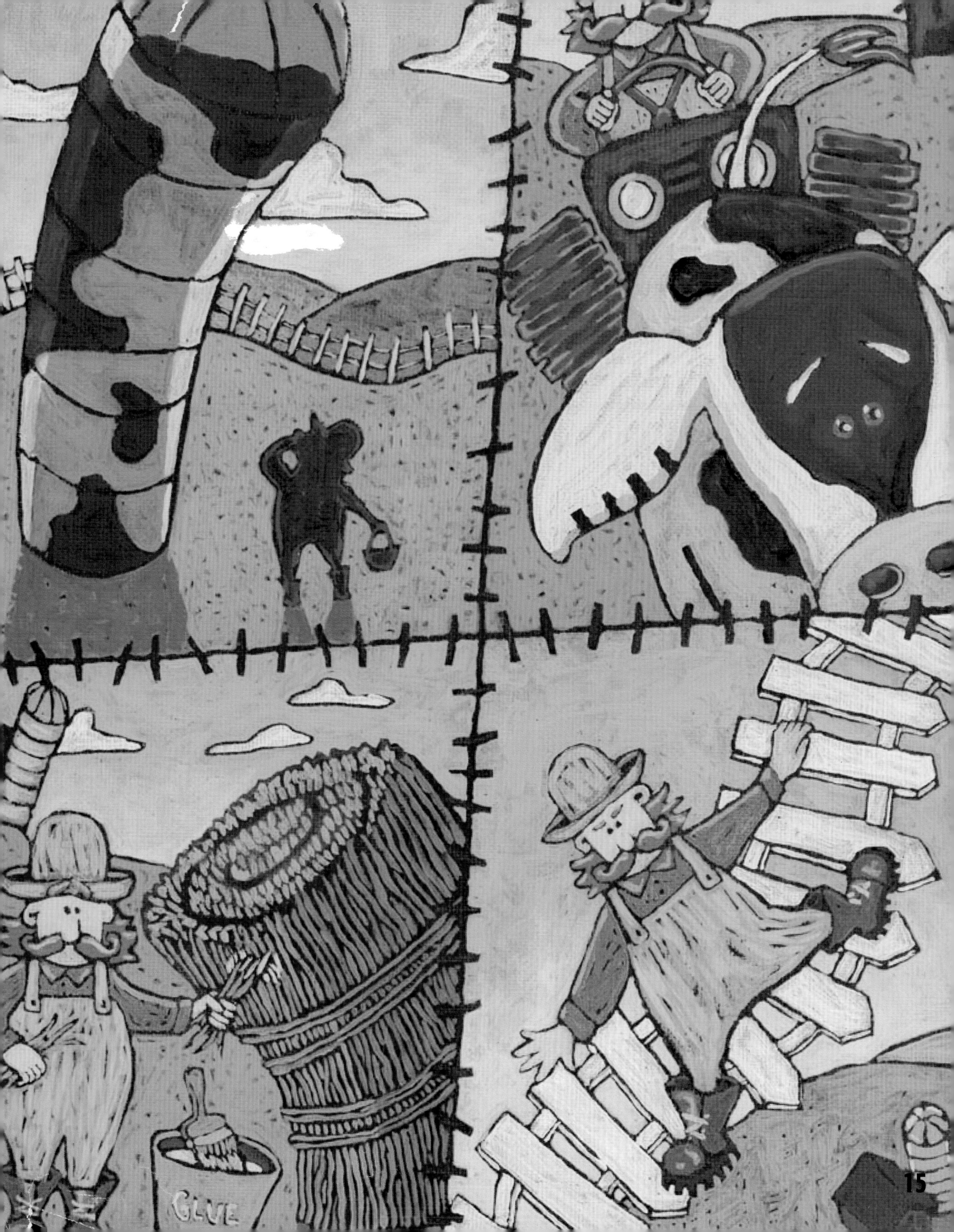
GLUE

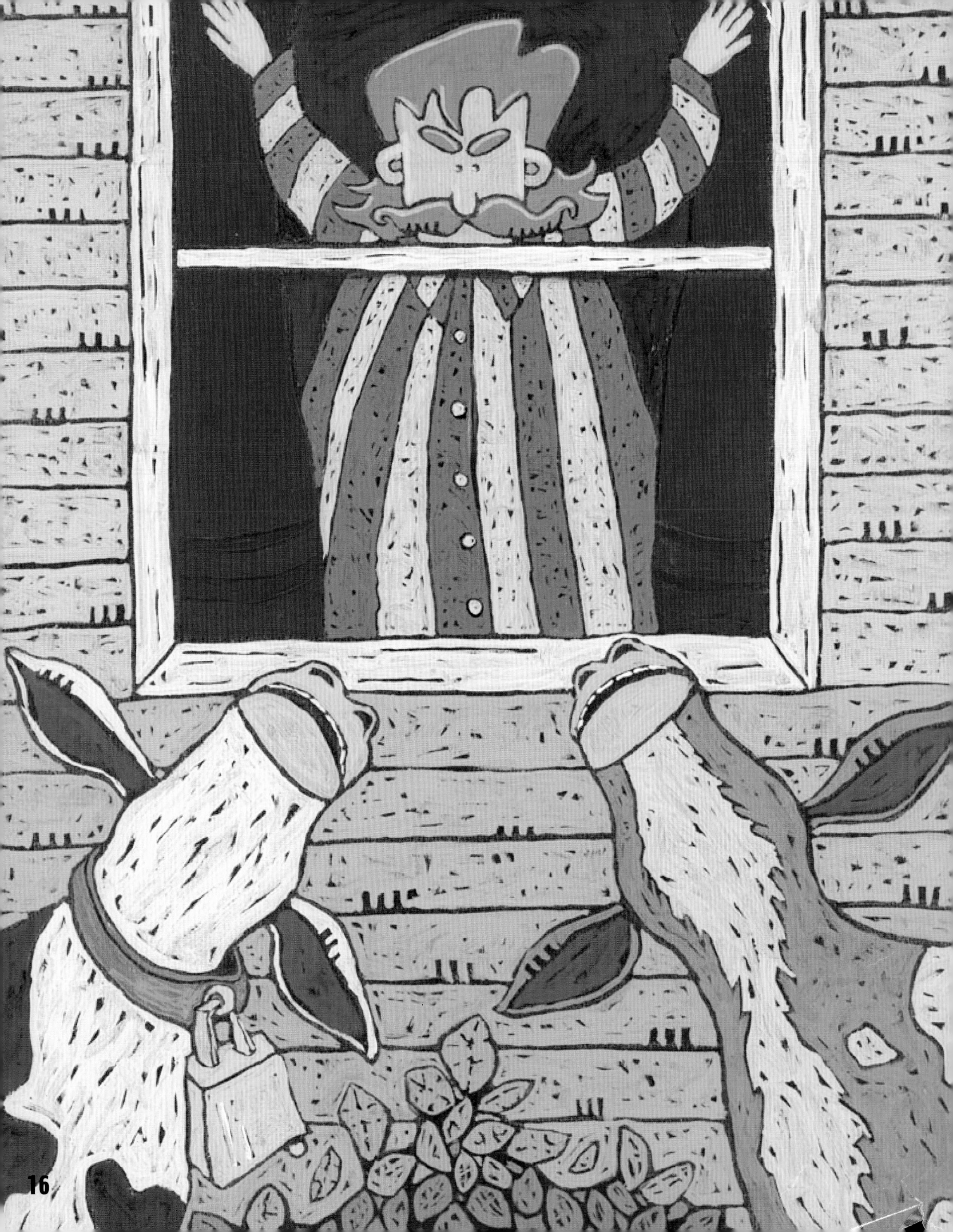

Mooooooo! Mooooooooo! Moooooooo!

Farmer Felandro sat up. "What's that noise?" he grumbled. Then he remembered: "Oh, crumps! I woke up the cows when I put the dogs in the hayloft. Now they will bellow all night long."

So the farmer stuck his feet into his old brown work boots and clumpidy clumped down the steps. He closed the screen door carefully on his way out and led the cows into their stalls.

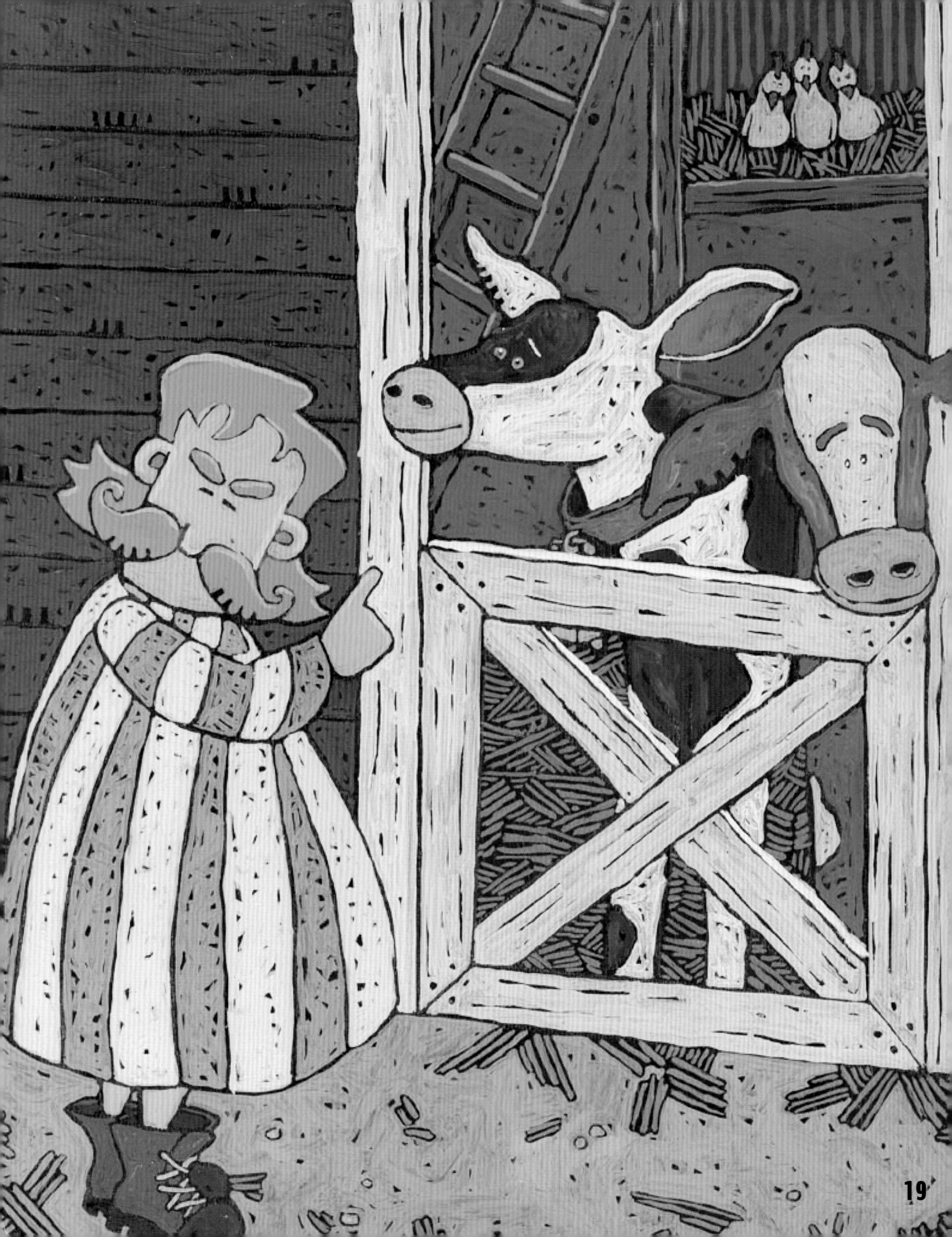

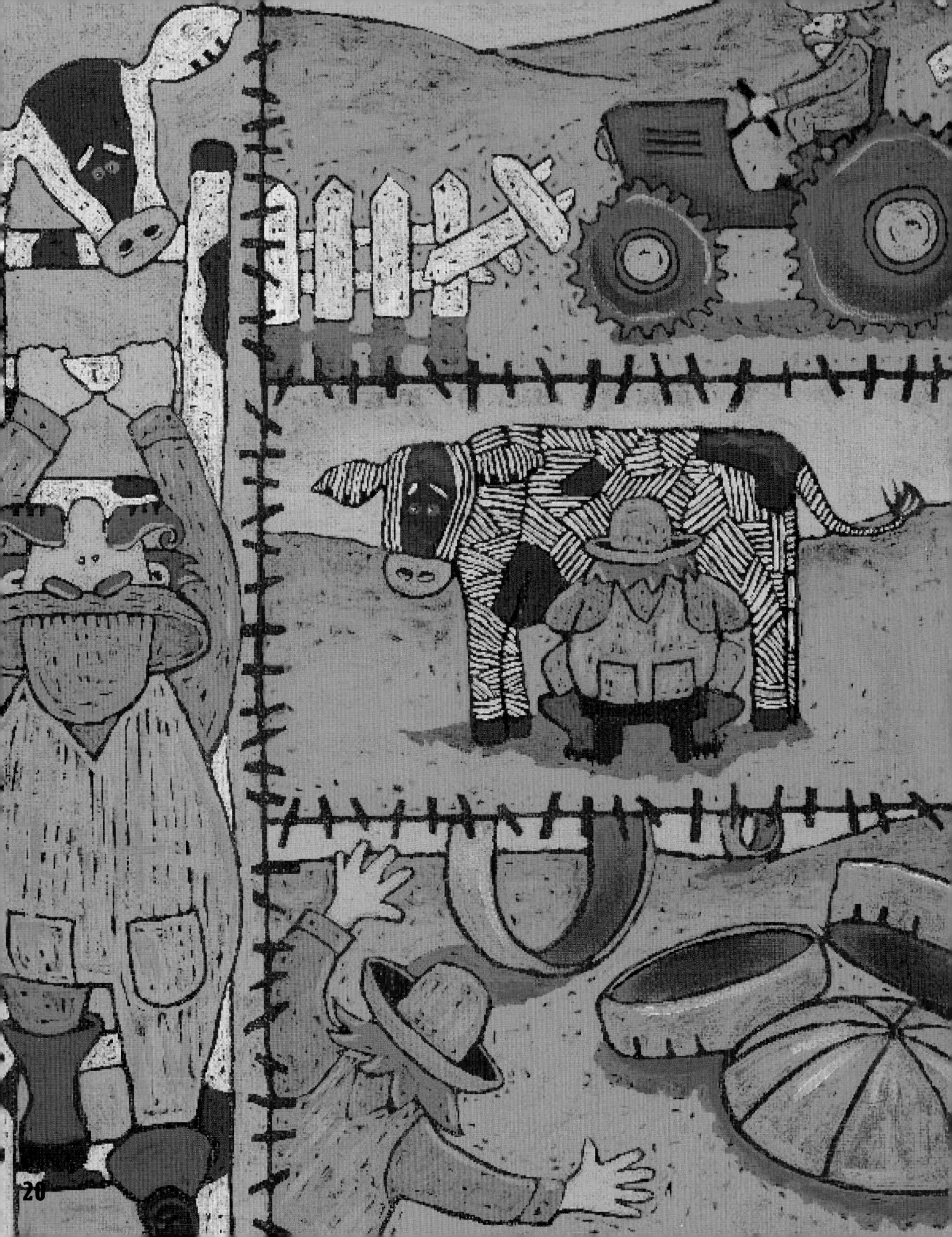

"Now it's quiet, and I can get some sleep." When he got back into bed, he pulled the blanket up under his nose and yawned.

"I am soooo tired. I can hardly think. Tomorrow will be a busy day. I have to climb the cow, mow the fence, milk the hay, and fix the silo. Morning comes early." Then he closed his sleepy eyes.

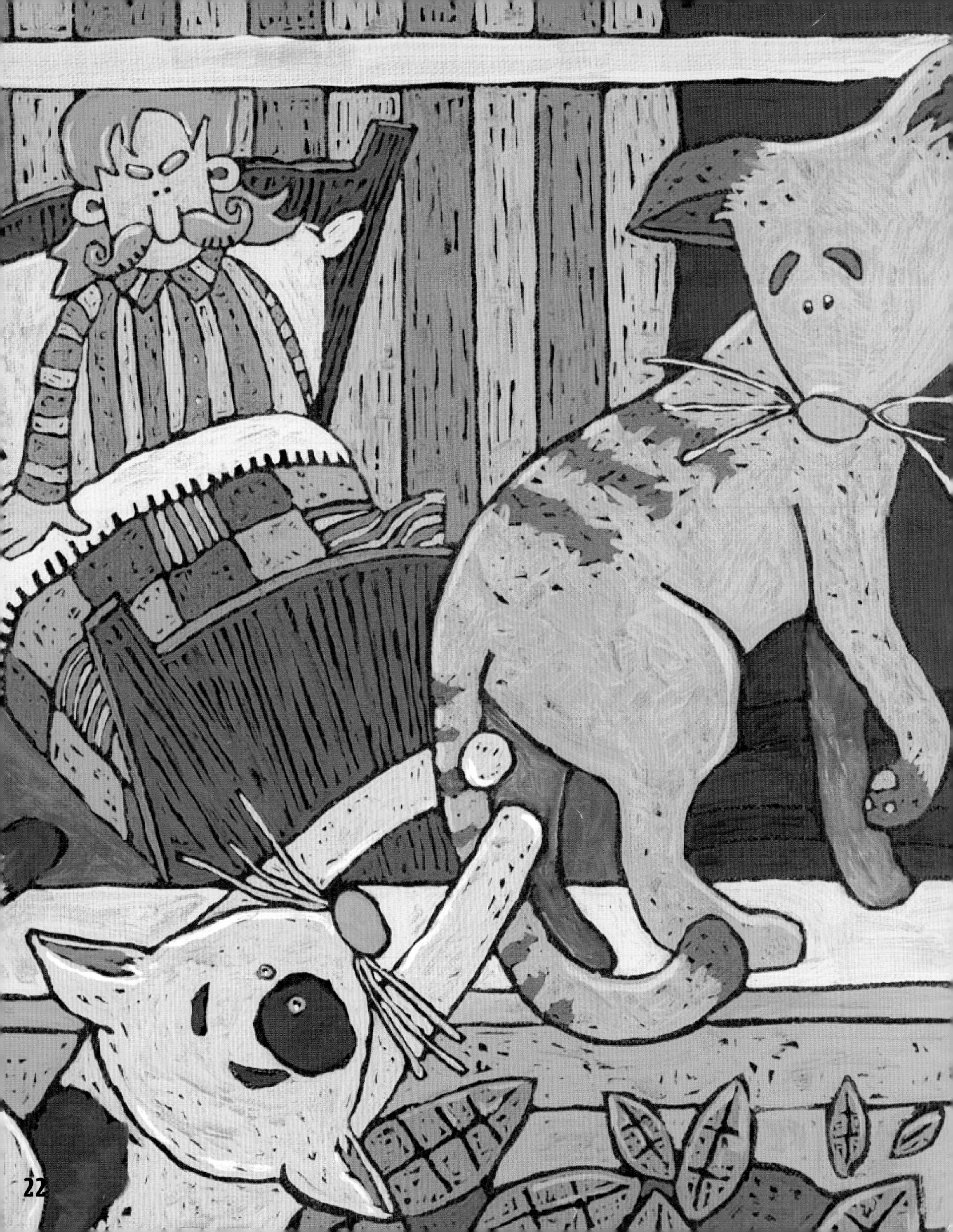

Meeeeyoweeee! Meeeyoweeee! Meeeyoweeee!

Farmer Felandro sat up. "What's that noise?" he grumbled. Then he remembered: "Oh, crumps! I woke up the cats when I put the cows in their stalls. Now they will fight all night long."

So the farmer stuck his feet into his old brown work boots and clumpidy clumped down the steps. He closed the screen door carefully on his way out and tried to chase the cats away. "I guess I need the dogs to help me," he said. So he let the dogs out of the hayloft.

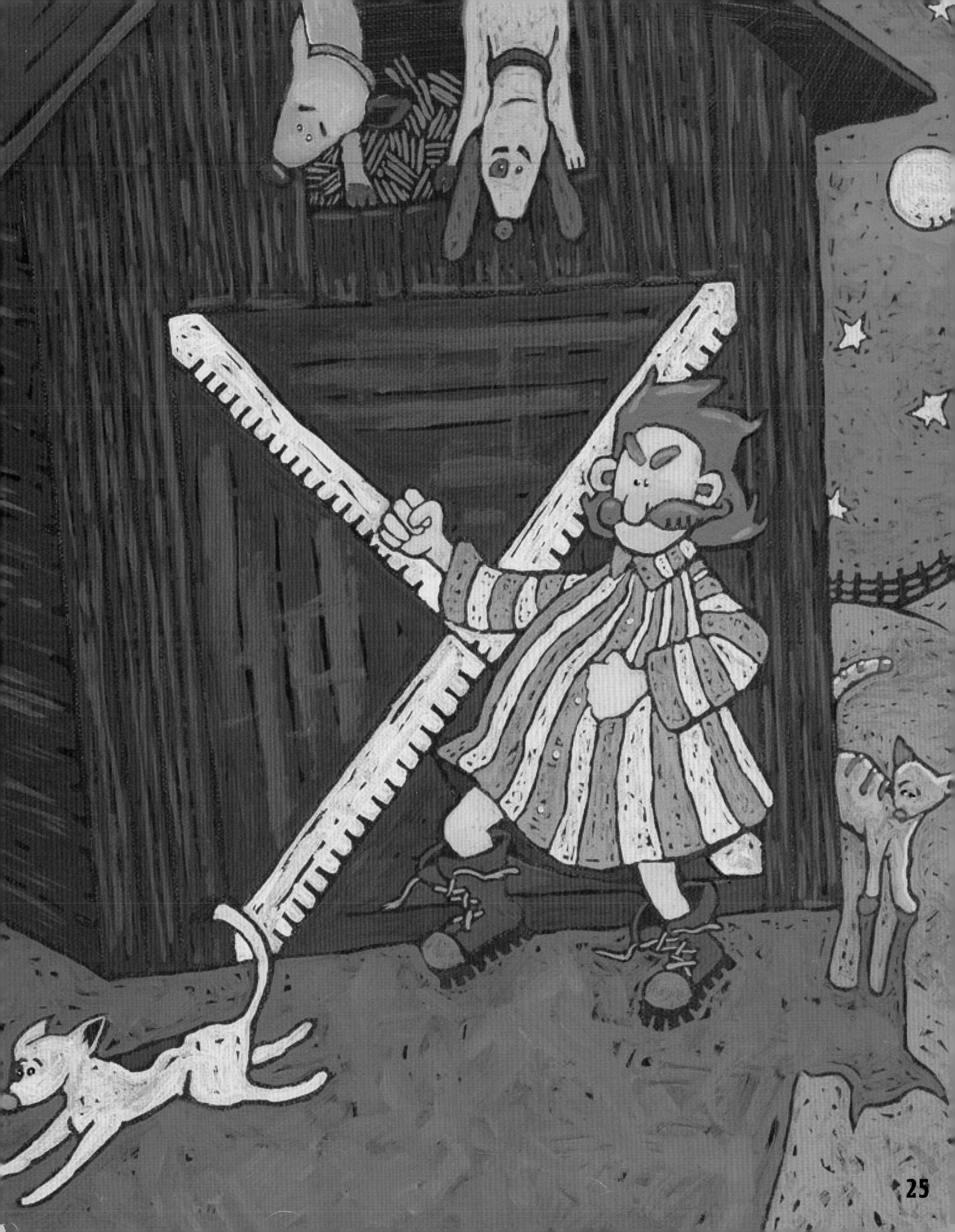

"Now it's quiet, and I can get some sleep." When he got back into bed, he pulled the blanket up under his nose and yawned.

"I am soooo tired. I can hardly think. Tomorrow will be a busy day. I have to fix the cow, climb the fence, milk the hay, and mow the silo. Morning comes early." Then he closed his sleepy eyes.

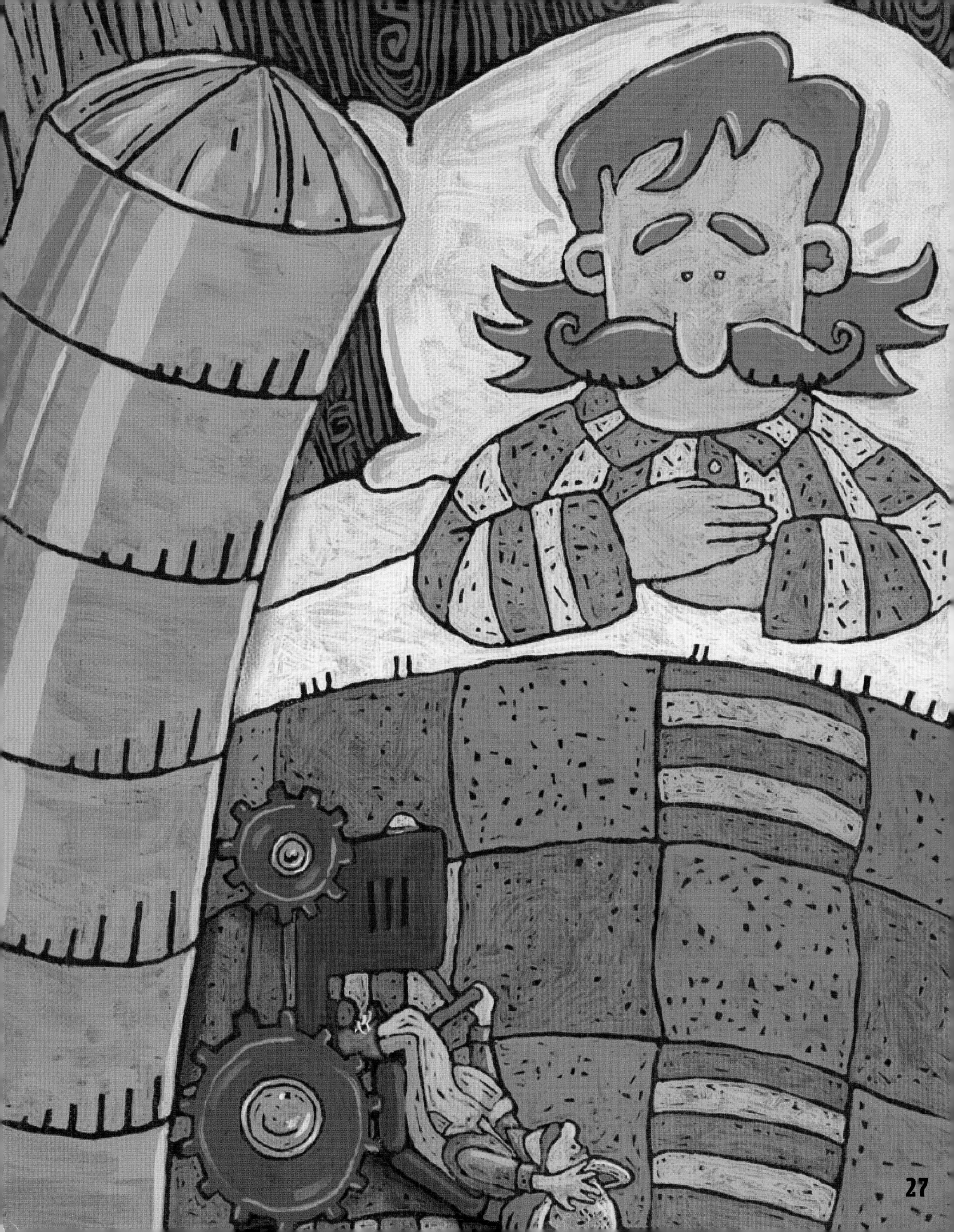

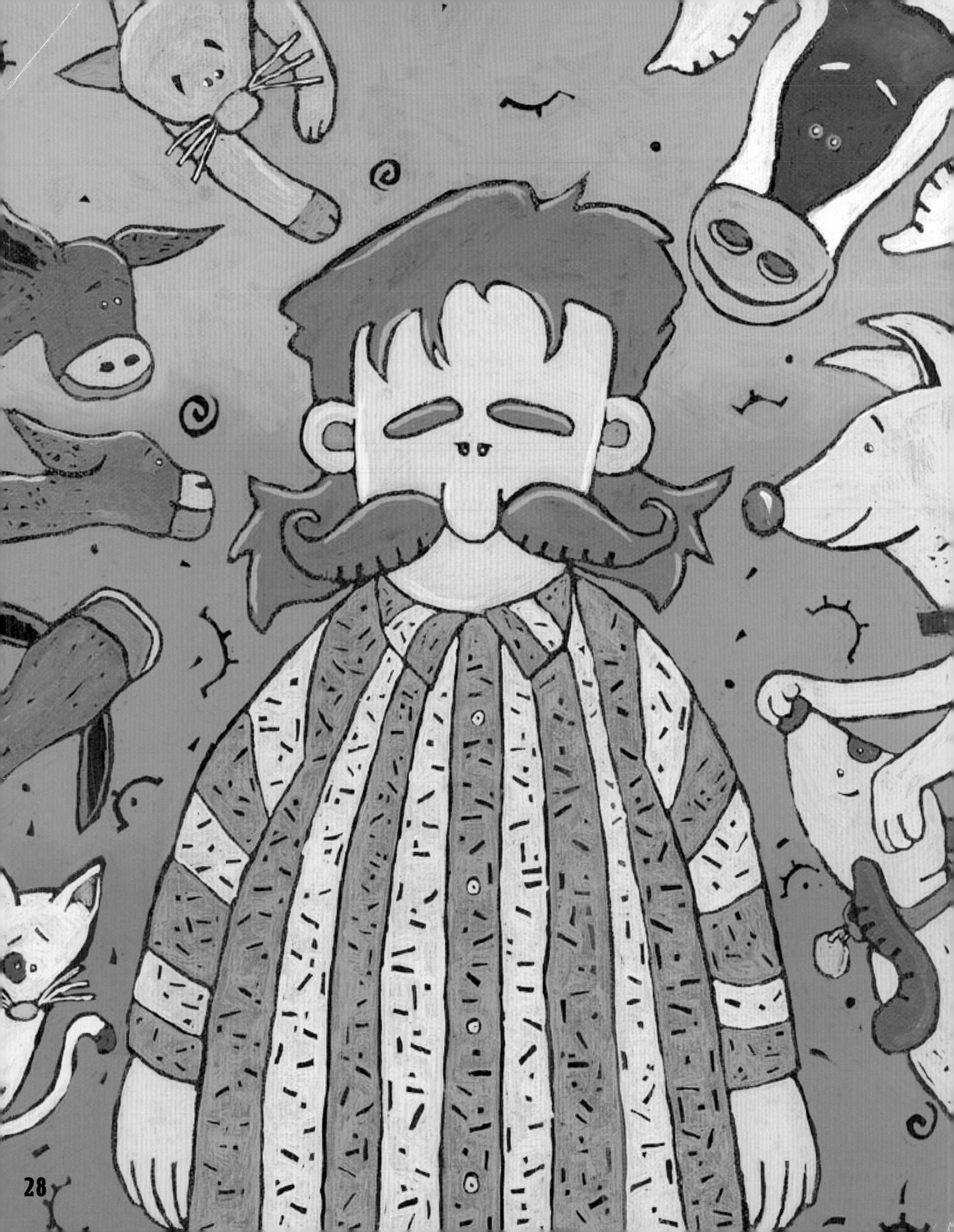

Burrrrufff! Burrrrufff! Burrrrufff!

Farmer Felandro sat up. "What's that noise?" he grumbled. Then he remembered: "Oh, crumps! I let the dogs out to chase the cats that woke up when I put the cows in the barn. The cows woke up when I put the dogs in the hayloft after they woke up when I put the kids in their pen. Now the dogs will bark all night long."

So the farmer stuck his feet into his old brown work boots and clumpidy clumped down the steps. He closed the screen door carefully. Then he started his day because morning had come.

And it **WAS** early.

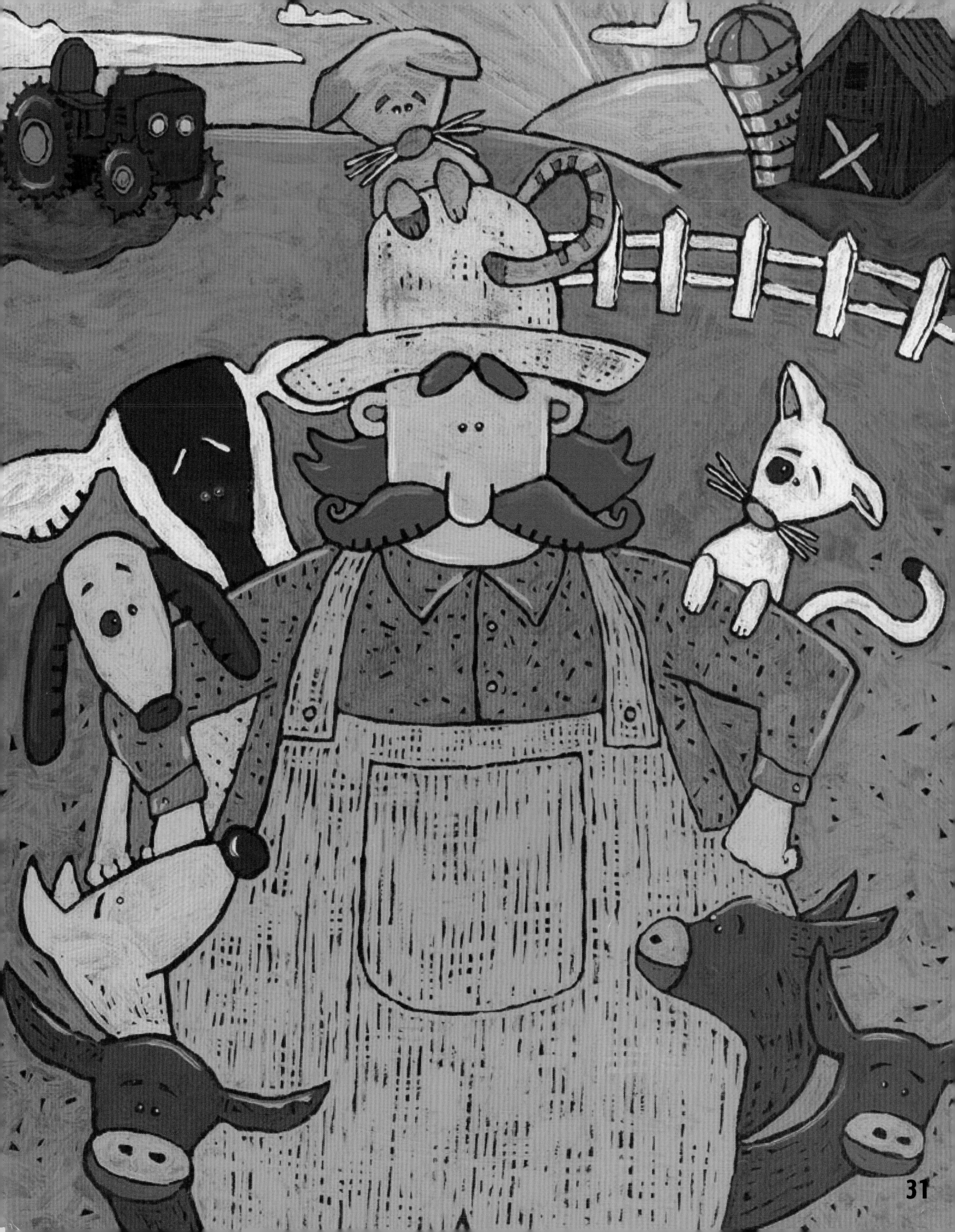